Friends

by

Lidia Ashton

2021

Balboa Press books may be ordered through booksellers or by contacting:

Balboa Press
A Division of Hay House
1663 Liberty Drive
Bloomington, IN 47403
www.balboapress.com.au
AU TFN: 1 800 844 925 (Toll Free inside Australia)
AU Local: 0283 107 086 (+61 2 8310 7086 from outside Australia)

Interior Image Credit: Images by Lidia Ashton, Peter Zenni and Weronika Stasiuk

ISBN: 978-1-9822-9281-2 (sc)
ISBN: 978-1-9822-9282-9 (e)

Print information available on the last page.

Balboa Press rev. date: 12/02/2021

BALBOA PRESS
A DIVISION OF HAY HOUSE

This book was written by myself for my Grandchildren however old they are.

To my Grandchildren
With Love
Babcia Ashton
2021

Silky

I am a Russian Blue cat
In France, they call me un chat
My tabby mate lost his cool
As there is nothing at home to do as a rule
He sleeps on the couch the whole day
Waiting for something to come close
To become his prey.

I love adventure and sunny days out
Not to stay home and wait for a pat
So, through the flap door and here I am
soaking the afternoon sun and looking for a game.
And here it is, the big tall tree,
is it enough mischief for me?

I jumped on the trunk and a few branches too
Hey, I can see you there, you little roo!
Another branch and one more too
Look at me now, THE BRAVE RUSSIAN BLUE.
I am at the top between the leaves
It is wonderful here, now I can get some peace.

My owner said before she left
If I stay home, I won't let her rest
Well, many a true word is said in jest
THIS IS MY STORY, ALL THE VERY BEST!

Luna the big dog

My name is Luna
And I am a big dog and your boss
So don't make me to be cross.
You are just two small kittens
who don't give a toss.

You are staying home today and behaving
I am ordering you as I am your boss.
Our parents are on a little break
and you are to be good as everything is at stake.
So, no scratching furniture, running
And climbing the kitchen bench
Stay placid and quiet before the brunch.
Our parents will return soon
to prepare our food
so, stay calm and don't act like a fool.

There is lots of traffic out there
Cars and trucks too.
If you engage in dangerous games
I will pay the consequences for your bad behavior case.
If you don't believe me
ask the mother of your friend the little roo.
It is safer to be out at night time for you
to climb the trees and jump the roofs.
Stay with me home now
For I know what to do and how
And I am the one who is wearing
the bosses' boots now.

Luna's Birthday

Hello to you all here
Did you know that
it is Luna's birthday today?
So, we are all gathered here
to make a plan to visit Luna,
to help celebrate with her.
Any ideas? Let's talk about them now
and remember we cannot let her down.
The presents may have to be wrapped soon
And the birthday hats to be worn too.
Luna's parents are making the special treats
for all of us and Luna's party it's going to be vast
so, you must be grateful and show good manners, I trust
There will be scones and muffins too
Your favorite, aren't they you little roo?.
Silky and his tiger looking mate organized lots of
games,
Isn't it great?!

Behave nicely and stay away from naughty pranks, and
when rewarded don't forget your thanks.
You may be given a little present to take home too
So, remember to bow and say thank you,
and when we are ready, we will sing.
Here we go, in a row
To a birthday party
Come on you, join the fun
Luna's birthday party has begun!

The best friends Excursion

Hello to you All again!
We are going to climb a hill today.
Through the small woods and
along the river and lake,
we will get to the top without a break.

Follow me then, I know this track well
as I come here often with Luna, Silky
and his tiger looking mate,
so, let's go and don't be afraid.

We will enter the forest through this gate.
Behind the gate a river runs freely,
when you look to the right
you will be able to see it clearly.

We will walk along and climb the peak
and then we will see the top of another hill, my dearies.
Trust me, we will be there soon to admire the view truly unique.
So, help each other to climb, if need be.
It is worth an effort to see this beautiful scenery.
And here it is, the peak, as beautiful as it can be! The beautiful greenery!

Find a place to sit and rest,
let me prepare the picnic, my very best!!
Congratulate yourself for reaching the crest,
as you my courageous friends won this quest,
And thank each other for being good, polite and helpful friends,
Always content,
And truly the best!!!

CPSIA information can be obtained
at www.ICGtesting.com
Printed in the USA
LVHW071637141221
706194LV00015B/778

9 781982 292812